1935<!-- obscured --> read a g<!-- obscured -->
either a lot of money or a library card.
Cheap paperbacks were available, but their
poor production generally mirrored the quality
between the covers. One weekend that year,
Allen Lane, Managing Director of The Bodley Head,
having spent the weekend visiting Agatha Christie,
found himself on a platform at Exeter station trying to
find something to read for his journey back to London.
He was appalled by the quality of the material he had to
choose from. Everything that Allen Lane achieved from that
day until his death in 1970 was based on a passionate belief
in the existence of 'a vast reading public for *intelligent*
books at a low price'. The result of his momentous vision
was the birth not only of Penguin, but of the 'paperback
revolution'. Quality writing became available for the price of
a packet of cigarettes, literature became a mass medium
for the first time, a nation of book-borrowers became a
nation of book-buyers – and the very concept of book
publishing was changed for ever. Those founding
principles – of quality and value, with an overarching
belief in the fundamental importance of reading –
have guided everything the company has
done since 1935. Sir Allen Lane's
pioneering spirit is still very much alive
at Penguin in 2005. Here's to
the next 70 years!

MORE THAN A BUSINESS

'We decided it was time to end the almost customary half-hearted manner in which cheap editions were produced – as though the only people who could possibly want cheap editions must belong to a lower order of intelligence. We, however, believed in the existence in this country of a vast reading public for intelligent books at a low price, and staked everything on it'
Sir Allen Lane, 1902–1970

'The Penguin Books are splendid value for sixpence, so splendid that if other publishers had any sense they would combine against them and suppress them'
George Orwell

'More than a business … a national cultural asset'
Guardian

'When you look at the whole Penguin achievement you know that it constitutes, in action, one of the more democratic successes of our recent social history'
Richard Hoggart

A Taste of the Unexpected

ROALD DAHL

PENGUIN BOOKS

PENGUIN BOOKS

Published by the Penguin Group
Penguin Books Ltd, 80 Strand, London WC2R ORL, England
Penguin Group (USA) Inc., 375 Hudson Street, New York, New York 10014, USA
Penguin Group (Canada), 10 Alcorn Avenue, Toronto, Ontario, Canada M4V 3B2
(a division of Pearson Penguin Canada Inc.)
Penguin Ireland, 25 St Stephen's Green, Dublin 2, Ireland
(a division of Penguin Books Ltd)
Penguin Group (Australia), 250 Camberwell Road, Camberwell, Victoria 3124,
Australia (a division of Pearson Australia Group Pty Ltd)
Penguin Books India Pvt Ltd, 11 Community Centre,
Panchsheel Park, New Delhi – 110 017, India
Penguin Group (NZ), cnr Airborne and Rosedale Roads, Albany,
Auckland 1310, New Zealand (a division of Pearson New Zealand Ltd)
Penguin Books (South Africa) (Pty) Ltd, 24 Sturdee Avenue,
Rosebank 2196, South Africa

Penguin Books Ltd, Registered Offices: 80 Strand, London WC2R ORL, England

www.penguin.com

'Taste' first published in *Someone Like You* by Secker & Warburg Ltd 1954
'The Landlady' and 'The Way Up To Heaven'
first published in *Kiss, Kiss* by Michael Joseph 1960
First published in one volume as *Completely Unexpected Tales* in Penguin Books 1986
This selection published as a Pocket Penguin 2005

1

Set in 11/13pt Monotype Dante
Typeset by Palimpsest Book Production Limited
Polmont, Stirlingshire
Printed in England by Clays Ltd, St Ives plc

Contents

Taste

There were six of us to dinner that night at Mike Schofield's house in London: Mike and his wife and daughter, my wife and I, and a man called Richard Pratt.

Richard Pratt was a famous gourmet. He was president of a small society known as the Epicures, and each month he circulated privately to its members a pamphlet on food and wines. He organized dinners where sumptuous dishes and rare wines were served. He refused to smoke for fear of harming his palate, and when discussing wine, he had a curious, rather droll habit of referring to it as though it were a living being. 'A prudent wine,' he would say, 'rather diffident and evasive, but quite prudent.' Or, 'A good-humoured wine, benevolent and cheerful – slightly obscene, perhaps, but none the less good-humoured.'

I had been to dinner at Mike's twice before when Richard Pratt was there, and on each occasion Mike and his wife had gone out of their way to produce a special meal for the famous gourmet. And this one, clearly, was to be no exception. The moment we entered the dining-room, I could see that the table was laid for a feast. The tall candles, the yellow roses, the quantity of shining silver, the three wineglasses to each person, and above all, the faint scent of roasting meat from the kitchen brought the first warm oozings of saliva to my mouth.

As we sat down, I remembered that on both Richard Pratt's previous visits Mike had played a little betting game with him over the claret, challenging him to name its breed and its vintage. Pratt had replied that that should not be too difficult provided it was one of the great years. Mike had then bet him a case of the wine in question that he could not do it. Pratt had accepted, and had won both times. Tonight I felt sure that the little game would be played over again, for Mike was quite willing to lose the bet in order to prove that his wine was good enough to be recognized, and Pratt, for his part, seemed to take a grave, restrained pleasure in displaying his knowledge.

The meal began with a plate of whitebait, fried very crisp in butter, and to go with it there was a Moselle. Mike got up and poured the wine himself, and when he sat down again, I could see that he was watching Richard Pratt. He had set the bottle in front of me so that I could read the label. It said, 'Geierslay Ohligsberg, 1945'. He leaned over and whispered to me that Geierslay was a tiny village in the Moselle, almost unknown outside Germany. He said that this wine we were drinking was something unusual, that the output of the vineyard was so small that it was almost impossible for a stranger to get any of it. He had visited Geierslay personally the previous summer in order to obtain the few dozen bottles that they had finally allowed him to have.

'I doubt whether anyone else in the country has any of it at the moment,' he said. I saw him glance again at Richard Pratt. 'Great thing about Moselle,' he continued, raising his voice, 'it's the perfect wine to serve before a claret. A lot of people serve a Rhine wine instead, but that's because they don't know any better. A Rhine wine will kill a delicate claret, you know that? It's barbaric to serve a Rhine before a claret. But a Moselle – ah! – a Moselle is exactly right.'

Mike Schofield was an amiable, middle-aged man. But he was a stockbroker. To be precise, he was a jobber in the stock market, and like a number of his kind, he seemed to be somewhat embarrassed, almost ashamed to find that he had made so much money with so slight a talent. In his heart he knew that he was not really much more than a bookmaker – an unctuous, infinitely respectable, secretly unscrupulous bookmaker – and he knew that his friends knew it, too. So he was seeking now to become a man of culture, to cultivate a literary and aesthetic taste, to collect paintings, music, books, and all the rest of it. His little sermon about Rhine wine and Moselle was a part of this thing, this culture that he sought.

'A charming little wine, don't you think?' he said. He was still watching Richard Pratt. I could see him give a rapid furtive glance down the table each time he dropped his head to take a mouthful of whitebait.

I could almost *feel* him waiting for the moment when Pratt would take his first sip, and look up from his glass with a smile of pleasure, of astonishment, perhaps even of wonder, and then there would be a discussion and Mike would tell him about the village of Geierslay.

But Richard Pratt did not taste his wine. He was completely engrossed in conversation with Mike's eighteen-year-old daughter, Louise. He was half turned towards her, smiling at her, telling her, so far as I could gather, some story about a chef in a Paris restaurant. As he spoke, he leaned closer and closer to her, seeming in his eagerness almost to impinge upon her, and the poor girl leaned as far as she could away from him, nodding politely, rather desperately, and looking not at his face but at the topmost button of his dinner jacket.

We finished our fish, and the maid came round removing the plates. When she came to Pratt, she saw that he had not yet touched his food, so she hesitated, and Pratt noticed her. He waved her away, broke off his conversation, and quickly began to eat, popping the little crisp brown fish quickly into his mouth with rapid jabbing movements of his fork. Then, when he had finished, he reached for his glass, and in two short swallows he tipped the wine down his throat and turned immediately to resume his conversation with Louise Schofield.

Mike saw it all. I was conscious of him sitting there, very still, containing himself, looking at his guest. His round jovial face seemed to loosen slightly and to sag, but he contained himself and was still and said nothing.

Soon the maid came forward with the second course. This was a large roast of beef. She placed it on the table in front of Mike who stood up and carved it, cutting the slices very thin, laying them gently on the plates for the maid to take around. When he had served everyone, including himself, he put down the carving knife and leaned forward with both hands on the edge of the table.

'Now,' he said, speaking to all of us but looking at Richard Pratt. 'Now for the claret. I must go and fetch the claret, if you'll excuse me.'

'You go and fetch it, Mike?' I said. 'Where is it?'

'In my study, with the cork out – breathing.'

'Why the study?'

'Acquiring room temperature, of course. It's been there twenty-four hours.'

'But why the study?'

'It's the best place in the house. Richard helped me choose it last time he was here.'

At the sound of his name, Pratt looked round.

'That's right, isn't it?' Mike said.

'Yes,' Pratt answered, nodding gravely. 'That's right.'

'On top of the green filing cabinet in my study,' Mike said. 'That's the place we chose. A good draught-free spot in a room with an even temperature. Excuse me now, will you, while I fetch it.'

The thought of another wine to play with had

5

restored his humour, and he hurried out of the door, to return a minute later more slowly, walking softly, holding in both hands a wine basket in which a dark bottle lay. The label was out of sight, facing downwards. 'Now!' he cried as he came towards the table. 'What about this one, Richard? You'll never name this one!'

Richard Pratt turned slowly and looked up at Mike, then his eyes travelled down to the bottle nestling in its small wicker basket, and he raised his eyebrows, a slight, supercilious arching of the brows, and with it a pushing outward of the wet lower lip, suddenly imperious and ugly.

'You'll never get it,' Mike said. 'Not in a hundred years.'

'A claret?' Richard Pratt asked, condescending.

'Of course.'

'I assume, then, that it's from one of the smaller vineyards?'

'Maybe it is, Richard. And then again, maybe it isn't.'

'But it's a good year? One of the great years?'

'Yes, I guarantee that.'

'Then it shouldn't be too difficult,' Richard Pratt said, drawling his words, looking exceedingly bored. Except that, to me, there was something strange about his drawling and his boredom: between the eyes a shadow of something evil, and in his bearing an intentness that gave me a faint sense of uneasiness as I watched him.

'This one is really rather difficult,' Mike said. 'I won't force you to bet on this one.'

'Indeed. And why not?' Again the slow arching of the brows, the cool, intent look.

'Because it's difficult.'

'That's not very complimentary to me, you know.'

'My dear man,' Mike said, 'I'll bet you with pleasure, if that's what you wish.'

'It shouldn't be too hard to name it.'

'You mean you want to bet?'

I'm perfectly willing to bet,' Richard Pratt said.

'All right then, we'll have the usual. A case of the wine itself.'

'You don't think I'll be able to name it, do you.'

'As a matter of fact, and with all due respect, I don't,' Mike said. He was making some effort to remain polite, but Pratt was not bothering overmuch to conceal his contempt for the whole proceeding. And yet, curiously, his next question seemed to betray a certain interest.

'You like to increase the bet?'

'No, Richard. A case is plenty.'

'Would you like to bet fifty cases?'

'That would be silly.'

Mike stood very still behind his chair at the head of the table, carefully holding the bottle in its ridiculous wicker basket. There was a trace of whiteness around his nostrils now, and his mouth was shut very tight.

Pratt was lolling back in his chair, looking up at him, the eyebrows raised, the eyes half closed, a little smile touching the corners of his lips. And again I saw, or thought I saw, something distinctly disturbing about the man's face, that shadow of intentness between the eyes, and in the eyes themselves, right in their centres where it was black, a small slow spark of shrewdness, hiding.

'So you don't want to increase the bet?'

'As far as I'm concerned, old man, I don't give a damn,' Mike said. 'I'll bet you anything you like.'

The three women and I sat quietly, watching the two men. Mike's wife was becoming annoyed; her mouth had gone sour and I felt that at any moment she was going to interrupt. Our roast beef lay before us on our plates, slowly steaming.

'So you'll bet me anything I like?'

'That's what I told you. I'll bet you anything you damn well please, if you want to make an issue out of it.'

'Even ten thousand pounds?'

'Certainly I will, if that's the way you want it.' Mike was more confident now. He knew quite well that he could call any sum Pratt cared to mention.

'So you say I can name the bet?' Pratt asked again.

'That's what I said.'

There was a pause while Pratt looked slowly around the table, first at me, then at the three women, each in turn. He appeared to be reminding us that we were witness to the offer.

'Mike!' Mrs Schofield said. 'Mike, why don't we stop this nonsense and eat our food. It's getting cold.'

'But it isn't nonsense,' Pratt told her evenly. 'We're making a little bet.'

I noticed the maid standing in the background holding a dish of vegetables, wondering whether to come forward with them or not.

'All right, then,' Pratt said, 'I'll tell you what I want you to bet.'

'Come on, then,' Mike said, rather reckless. 'I don't give a damn what it is – you're on.'

Pratt nodded, and again the little smile moved the corners of his lips, and then, quite slowly, looking at Mike all the time, he said, 'I want you to bet me the hand of your daughter in marriage.'

Louise Schofield gave a jump. 'Hey!' she cried. 'No! That's not funny! Look here, Daddy, that's not funny at all.'

'No, dear,' her mother said. 'They're only joking.'

'I'm not joking,' Richard Pratt said.

'It's ridiculous,' Mike said. He was off balance again now.

'You said you'd bet anything I liked.'

'I meant money.'

'You didn't *say* money.'

'That's what I meant.'

'Then it's a pity you didn't say it. But anyway, if you wish to go back on your offer, that's quite all right with me.'

'It's not a question of going back on my offer, old man. It's a no-bet anyway, because you can't match the stake. You yourself don't happen to have a daughter to put up against mine in case you lose. And if you had, I wouldn't want to marry her.'

'I'm glad of that, dear,' his wife said.

'I'll put up anything you like,' Pratt announced. 'My house, for example. How about my house?'

'Which one?' Mike asked, joking now.

'The country one.'

'Why not the other one as well?'

'All right then, if you wish it. Both my houses.'

At that point I saw Mike pause. He took a step forward and placed the bottle in its basket gently down on the table. He moved the salt-cellar to one side, then the pepper, and then he picked up his knife, studied the blade thoughtfully for a moment, and put it down again. His daughter, too, had seen him pause.

'Now, Daddy!' she cried. 'Don't be *absurd*! It's *too* silly for words. I refuse to be betted on like this.'

'Quite right, dear,' her mother said. 'Stop it at once, Mike, and sit down and eat your food.'

Mike ignored her. He looked over at his daughter and he smiled, a slow, fatherly, protective smile. But in his eyes, suddenly, there glimmered a little triumph. 'You know,' he said, smiling as he spoke. 'You know, Louise, we ought to think about this a bit.'

'Now, stop it, Daddy! I refuse even to listen to you! Why, I've never heard anything so ridiculous in my life!'

'No, seriously, my dear. Just wait a moment and hear what I have to say.'

'But I don't *want* to hear it.'

'Louise! Please! It's like this. Richard, here, has offered us a serious bet. He is the one who wants to make it, not me. And if he loses, he will have to hand over a considerable amount of property. Now, wait a minute, my dear, don't interrupt. The point is this. *He cannot possibly win.*'

'He seems to think he can.'

'Now listen to me, because I know what I'm talking about. The expert, when tasting a claret – so long as it is not one of the famous great wines like Lafite or Latour – can only get a certain way towards naming the vineyard. He can, of course, tell you the Bordeaux district from which the wine comes, whether it is from St Emilion, Pomerol, Graves, or Médoc. But then each district has several communes, little counties, and each county has many, many small vineyards. It is impossible for a man to differentiate between them all by taste and smell alone. I don't mind telling you that this one I've got here is a wine from a small vineyard that is surrounded by many other small vineyards, and he'll never get it. It's impossible.'

'You can't be sure of that,' his daughter said.

'I'm telling you I can. Though I say it myself, I understand quite a bit about this wine business, you know. And anyway, heavens alive, girl, I'm your father and you don't think I'd let you in for – for something you didn't want, do you? I'm trying to make you some money.'

'Mike!' his wife said sharply. 'Stop it now, Mike, please!'

Again he ignored her. 'If you will take this bet,' he said to his daughter, 'in ten minutes you will be the owner of two large houses.'

'But I don't want two large houses, Daddy.'

'Then sell them. Sell them back to him on the spot. I'll arrange all that for you. And then, just think of it, my dear, you'll be rich! You'll be independent for the rest of your life!'

'Oh, Daddy, I don't like it. I think it's silly.'

'So do I,' the mother said. She jerked her head briskly up and down as she spoke, like a hen. 'You ought to be ashamed of yourself, Michael, ever suggesting such a thing! Your own daughter, too!'

Mike didn't even look at her. 'Take it!' he said eagerly, staring hard at the girl. 'Take it, quick! I'll guarantee you won't lose.'

'But I don't like it, Daddy.'

'Come on, girl. Take it!'

Mike was pushing her hard. He was leaning towards her, fixing her with two hard bright eyes, and it was not easy for the daughter to resist him.

'But what if I lose?'

'I keep telling you, you can't lose. I'll guarantee it.'

'Oh, Daddy, must I?'

'I'm making you a fortune. So come on now. What do you say, Louise? All right?'

For the last time, she hesitated. Then she gave a helpless little shrug of the shoulders and said, 'Oh, all right, then. Just so long as you swear there's no danger of losing.'

'Good!' Mike cried. 'That's fine! Then it's a bet!'

'Yes,' Richard Pratt said, looking at the girl. 'It's a bet.'

Immediately, Mike picked up the wine, tipped the first thimbleful into his own glass, then skipped excitedly around the table filling up the others. Now everyone was watching Richard Pratt, watching his face as he reached slowly for his glass with his right hand and lifted it to his nose. The man was about fifty years old and he did not have a pleasant face. Somehow, it was all mouth – mouth and lips – the full, wet lips of the professional gourmet, the lower lip hanging downward in the centre, a pendulous, permanently open taster's lip, shaped open to receive the rim of a glass or a morsel of food. Like a keyhole, I thought, watching it; his mouth is like a large wet keyhole.

Slowly he lifted the glass to his nose. The point of the nose entered the glass and moved over the surface of the wine, delicately sniffing. He swirled the wine gently around in the glass to receive the bouquet. His concentration was intense. He had closed his eyes, and now the whole top half of his body, the head and neck and chest, seemed to become a kind of huge sensitive smelling-machine, receiving, filtering, analysing the message from the sniffing nose.

Mike, I noticed, was lounging in his chair, apparently unconcerned, but he was watching every move. Mrs Schofield, the wife, sat prim and upright at the other end of the table, looking straight ahead, her face tight with disapproval. The daughter, Louise, had shifted her chair away a little, and sidewise, facing the gourmet, and she, like her father, was watching closely.

For at least a minute, the smelling process continued; then, without opening his eyes or moving his head, Pratt lowered the glass to his mouth and tipped in almost half the contents. He paused, his mouth full of wine, getting the first taste; then, he permitted some of it to trickle down his throat and I saw his Adam's apple move as it passed by. But most of it he retained in his mouth. And now, without swallowing again, he drew in through his lips a thin breath of air which mingled with the fumes of the wine in the mouth and passed on down into his lungs. He held the breath, blew it out through his nose, and finally began to roll the wine around under the tongue, and chewed it, actually chewed it with his teeth as though it were bread.

It was a solemn, impassive performance, and I must say he did it well.

'Um,' he said, putting down the glass, running a pink tongue over his lips. 'Um – yes. A very interesting little wine – gentle and gracious, almost feminine in the after-taste.'

There was an excess of saliva in his mouth, and as he spoke he spat an occasional bright speck of it on to the table.

'Now we can start to eliminate,' he said. 'You will pardon me for doing this carefully, but there is much at stake. Normally I would perhaps take a bit of a chance, leaping forward quickly and landing right in the middle of the vineyard of my choice. But this time – I must move cautiously this time, must I not?' He looked up at Mike and smiled, a thick-lipped, wet-lipped smile. Mike did not smile back.

'First, then, which district in Bordeaux does this wine come from? That's not too difficult to guess. It is far too light in the body to be from either St Emilion or Graves. It is obviously a Médoc. There's no doubt about *that*.

'Now – from which commune in Médoc does it come? That also, by elimination, should not be too difficult to decide. Margaux? No. It cannot be Margaux. It has not the violent bouquet of a Margaux. Pauillac? It cannot be Pauillac, either. It is too tender, too gentle and wistful for Pauillac. The wine of Pauillac has a character that is almost imperious in its taste. And also, to me, a Pauillac contains just a little pith, a curious dusty, pithy flavour that the grape acquires from the soil of the district. No, no. This – this is a very gentle wine, demure and bashful in the first taste, emerging shyly but quite graciously in the second. A little arch, perhaps, in the second taste, and a little naughty also, teasing the tongue with a trace, just a trace of tannin. Then, in the after-taste, delightful – consoling and feminine, with a certain blithely generous quality that one associates only with the wines of the commune of St Julien. Unmistakably this is a St Julien.'

He leaned back in his chair, held his hands up level with his chest, and placed the fingertips carefully together. He was becoming ridiculously pompous, but I thought that some of it was deliberate, simply to mock his host. I found myself waiting rather tensely for him to go on. The girl Louise was lighting a cigarette. Pratt heard the match strike and he turned to her, flaring suddenly with real anger. 'Please!' he said. 'Please don't do that! It's a disgusting habit, to smoke at table!'

She looked up at him, still holding the burning match in one hand, the big slow eyes settling on his face, resting there a moment, moving away again, slow and contemptuous. She bent her head and blew out the match, but continued to hold the unlighted cigarette in her fingers.

'I'm sorry, my dear,' Pratt said, 'but I simply cannot have smoking at table.'

She didn't look at him again.

'Now, let me see – where were we?' he said. 'Ah, yes. This wine is from Bordeaux, from the commune of St Julien, in the district of Médoc. So far, so good. But now we come to the more difficult part – the name of the vineyard itself. For in St Julien there are many vineyards, and as our host so rightly remarked earlier on, there is often not much difference between the wine of one and the wine of another. But we shall see.'

He paused again, closing his eyes. 'I am trying to establish the "growth",' he said. 'If I can do that, it will be half the battle. Now, let me see. This wine is obviously not from a first-growth vineyard – nor even a second. It is not a great wine. The quality, the – the – what do you call it? – the radiance, the power, is lacking. But a third growth – that it could be. And yet I doubt it. We know it is a good year – our host has said so – and this is probably flattering it a little bit. I must be careful. I must be very careful here.'

He picked up his glass and took another small sip.

'Yes,' he said, sucking his lips, 'I was right. It is a fourth growth. Now I am sure of it. A fourth growth from a very good year – from a great year, in fact. And that's what made it taste for a moment like a third – or even a second-growth wine. Good! That's better! Now we are closing in! What are the fourth-growth vineyards in the commune of St Julien?'

Again he paused, took up his glass, and held the rim against that sagging, pendulous lower lip of his. Then I saw the tongue shoot out, pink and narrow, the tip of it dipping into the wine, withdrawing swiftly again – a repulsive sight. When he lowered the glass, his eyes remained closed, the face concentrated, only the lips moving, sliding over each other like two pieces of wet, spongy rubber.

'There it is again!' he cried. 'Tannin in the middle taste, and the quick astringent squeeze upon the tongue. Yes, yes, of course! Now I have it! The wine comes from one of those small vineyards around Beychevelle. I remember now. The Beychevelle district, and the river and the little harbour that has silted up so the wine ships can no longer use it. Beychevelle . . . could it actually be a Beychevelle itself? No, I don't think so. Not quite. But it is somewhere very close. Château Talbot? Could it be Talbot? Yes, it could. Wait one moment.'

He sipped the wine again, and out of the side of my eye I noticed Mike Schofield and how he was leaning farther and farther forward over the table, his mouth slightly open, his small eyes fixed upon Richard Pratt.

'No. I was wrong. It is not a Talbot. A Talbot comes forward to you just a little quicker than this one, the fruit is nearer the surface. If it is a '34, which I believe it is, then it couldn't be Talbot. Well, well. Let me think. It is not a Beychevelle and it is not a Talbot, and yet – yet it is so close to both of them, so close, that the vineyard must be almost in between. Now, which could that be?'

He hesitated, and we waited, watching his face. Everyone, even Mike's wife, was watching him now. I heard the maid put down the dish of vegetables on the sideboard behind me, gently, so as not to disturb the silence.

'Ah!' he cried. 'I have it! Yes, I think I have it!'

For the last time, he sipped the wine. Then, still holding the glass up near his mouth, he turned to Mike and he smiled, a slow, silky smile, and he said, 'You know what this is? This is the little Château Branaire-Ducru.'

Mike sat tight, not moving.

'And the year, 1934.'

We all looked at Mike, waiting for him to turn the bottle around in its basket and show the label.

'Is that your final answer?' Mike said.

'Yes, I think so.'

'Well, is it or isn't it?'

'Yes, it is.'

'What was the name again?'

'Château Branaire-Ducru. Pretty little vineyard. Lovely old château. Know it quite well. Can't think why I didn't recognize it at once.'

'Come on, Daddy,' the girl said. 'Turn it round and let's have a peek. I want my two houses.'

'Just a minute,' Mike said. 'Wait just a minute.' He was sitting very quiet, bewildered-looking, and his face was becoming puffy and pale, as though all the force was draining slowly out of him.

'Michael!' his wife called sharply from the other end of the table. 'What's the matter?'

'Keep out of this, Margaret, will you please.'

Richard Pratt was looking at Mike, smiling with his mouth, his eyes small and bright. Mike was not looking at anyone.

'Daddy!' the daughter cried, agonized. 'But, Daddy, you don't mean to say he's guessed it right!'

'Now, stop worrying, my dear,' Mike said. 'There's nothing to worry about.'

I think it was more to get away from his family than anything else that Mike then turned to Richard Pratt and said, 'I'll tell you what, Richard. I think you and I better slip off into the next room and have a little chat.'

'I don't want a little chat,' Pratt said. 'All I want is to see the label on that bottle.' He knew he was a winner now; he had the bearing, the quiet arrogance of a winner, and I could see that he was prepared to become thoroughly nasty if there was any trouble. 'What are you waiting for?' he said to Mike. 'Go on and turn it round.'

Then this happened: the maid, the tiny, erect figure of the maid in her white-and-black uniform, was standing beside Richard Pratt, holding something out in her hand. 'I believe these are yours, sir,' she said.

Pratt glanced around, saw the pair of thin horn-rimmed spectacles that she held out to him, and for a moment he hesitated. 'Are they? Perhaps they are, I don't know.'

'Yes, sir, they're yours.' The maid was an elderly woman – nearer seventy than sixty – a faithful family retainer of many years' standing. She put the spectacles down on the table beside him.

Without thanking her, Pratt took them up and slipped them into his top pocket, behind the white handkerchief.

But the maid didn't go away. She remained standing beside and slightly behind Richard Pratt, and there was something so unusual in her manner and in the way she stood there, small, motionless and erect, that I for one found myself watching her with a sudden apprehension. Her old grey face had a frosty, determined look, the lips were compressed, the little chin was out, and the hands were clasped together tight before her. The curious cap on her head and the flash of white down the front of her uniform made her seem like some tiny, ruffled, white-breasted bird.

'You left them in Mr Schofield's study,' she said. Her voice was unnaturally, deliberately polite. 'On top of the green filing cabinet in his study, sir, when you happened to go in there by yourself before dinner.'

It took a few moments for the full meaning of her words to penetrate, and in the silence that followed I became aware of Mike and how he was slowly drawing himself up in his chair, and the colour coming to his face, and the eyes opening wide, and the curl of the mouth, and the dangerous little patch of whiteness beginning to spread around the area of the nostrils.

'Now, Michael!' his wife said. 'Keep calm now, Michael, dear! Keep calm!'

The Way Up To Heaven

All her life, Mrs Foster had had an almost pathologic-
al fear of missing a train, a plane, a boat, or even a
theatre curtain. In other respects, she was not a particu-
larly nervous woman, but the mere thought of
being late on occasions like these would throw her
into such a state of nerves that she would begin to
twitch. It was nothing much – just a tiny vellicating
muscle in the corner of the left eye, like a secret wink
– but the annoying thing was that it refused to disap-
pear until an hour or so after the train or plane or
whatever it was had been safely caught.

It was really extraordinary how in certain people
a simple apprehension about a thing like catching a
train can grow into a serious obsession. At least half
an hour before it was time to leave the house for the
station, Mrs Foster would step out of the elevator all
ready to go, with hat and coat and gloves, and then,
being quite unable to sit down, she would flutter and
fidget about from room to room until her husband,
who must have been well aware of her state, finally
emerged from his privacy and suggested in a cool dry
voice that perhaps they had better get going now, had
they not?

Mr Foster may possibly have had a right to be

irritated by this foolishness of his wife's, but he could have had no excuse for increasing her misery by keeping her waiting unnecessarily. Mind you, it is by no means certain that this is what he did, yet whenever they were to go somewhere, his timing was so accurate – just a minute or two late, you understand – and his manner so bland that it was hard to believe he wasn't purposely inflicting a nasty private little torture of his own on the unhappy lady. And one thing he must have known – that she would never dare to call out and tell him to hurry. He had disciplined her too well for that. He must also have known that if he was prepared to wait even beyond the last moment of safety, he could drive her nearly into hysterics. On one or two special occasions in the later years of their married life, it seemed almost as though he had *wanted* to miss the train simply in order to intensify the poor woman's suffering.

Assuming (though one cannot be sure) that the husband was guilty, what made his attitude doubly unreasonable was the fact that, with the exception of this one small irrepressible foible, Mrs Foster was and always had been a good and loving wife. For over thirty years, she had served him loyally and well. There was no doubt about this. Even she, a very modest woman, was aware of it, and although she had for years refused to let herself believe that Mr Foster would ever consciously torment her, there had been times recently when she had caught herself beginning to wonder.

Mr Eugene Foster, who was nearly seventy years old, lived with his wife in a large six-storey house in New York City, on East Sixty-second Street, and they had four servants. It was a gloomy place, and few people came to visit them. But on this particular morning in January, the house had come alive and there was a great deal of bustling about. One maid was distributing bundles of dust sheets to every room, while another was draping them over the furniture. The butler was bringing down suitcases and putting them in the hall. The cook kept popping up from the kitchen to have a word with the butler, and Mrs Foster herself, in an old-fashioned fur coat and with a black hat on top of her head, was flying from room to room and pretending to supervise these operations. Actually, she was thinking of nothing at all except that she was going to miss her plane if her husband didn't come out of his study soon and get ready.

'What time is it, Walker?' she said to the butler as she passed him.

'It's ten minutes past nine, Madam.'

'And has the car come?'

'Yes, Madam, it's waiting. I'm just going to put the luggage in now.'

'It takes an hour to get to Idlewild,' she said. 'My plane leaves at eleven. I have to be there half an hour beforehand for the formalities. I shall be late. I just *know* I'm going to be late.'

'I think you have plenty of time, Madam,' the butler

said kindly. 'I warned Mr Foster that you must leave at nine-fifteen. There's still another five minutes.'

'Yes, Walker, I know, I know. But get the luggage in quickly, will you please?'

She began walking up and down the hall, and whenever the butler came by, she asked him the time. This, she kept telling herself, was the *one* plane she must not miss. It had taken months to persuade her husband to allow her to go. If she missed it, he might easily decide that she should cancel the whole thing. And the trouble was that he insisted on coming to the airport to see her off.

'Dear God,' she said aloud, 'I'm going to miss it. I know, I know, I *know* I'm going to miss it.' The little muscle beside the left eye was twitching madly now. The eyes themselves were very close to tears.

'What time is it, Walker?'

'It's eighteen minutes past, Madam.'

'Now I really *will* miss it!' she cried. 'Oh, I wish he would come!'

This was an important journey for Mrs Foster. She was going all alone to Paris to visit her daughter, her only child, who was married to a Frenchman. Mrs Foster didn't much care for the Frenchman, but she was fond of her daughter, and, more than that, she had developed a great yearning to set eyes on her three grandchildren. She knew them only from the many photographs that she had received and that she kept putting up all over the house. They were beautiful, these children. She doted on them, and each time a new picture arrived she would carry it away and sit with it for a long time, staring at it lovingly and searching the small faces for signs of that old satisfying blood likeness that meant so much. And now, lately, she had come more and more to feel that she did not really wish to live out her days in a place where she could not be near her children, and have them visit her, and take them for walks, and buy them presents, and watch them grow. She knew, of course, that it was wrong and in a way disloyal to have thoughts like these while her husband was still alive. She knew also that although he was no longer active in his many enterprises, he would never consent to leave New York and live in Paris. It was a miracle that he had ever agreed to let her fly over there alone for six weeks to visit them. But, oh, how she wished she could live there always, and be close to them!

'Walker, what time is it?'

'Twenty-two minutes past, Madam.'

As he spoke, a door opened and Mr Foster came into the hall. He stood for a moment, looking intently at his wife, and she looked back at him – at this diminutive but still quite dapper old man with the huge bearded face that bore such an astonishing resemblance to those old photographs of Andrew Carnegie.

'Well,' he said, 'I suppose perhaps we'd better get going fairly soon if you want to catch that plane.'

'*Yes*, dear – *yes*! Everthing's ready. The car's waiting.'

'That's good,' he said. With his head over to one

26

side, he was watching her closely. He had a peculiar way of cocking the head and then moving it in a series of small, rapid jerks. Because of this and because he was clasping his hands up high in front of him, near the chest, he was somehow like a squirrel standing there – a quick clever old squirrel from the Park.

'Here's Walker with your coat, dear. Put it on.'

'I'll be with you in a moment,' he said. 'I'm just going to wash my hands.'

She waited for him, and the tall butler stood beside her, holding the coat and the hat.

'Walker, will I miss it?'

'No, Madam,' the butler said. 'I think you'll make it all right.'

Then Mr Foster appeared again, and the butler helped him on with his coat. Mrs Foster hurried outside and got into the hired Cadillac. Her husband came after her, but he walked down the steps of the house slowly, pausing halfway to observe the sky and to sniff the cold morning air.

'It looks a bit foggy,' he said as he sat down beside her in the car. 'And it's always worse out there at the airport. I shouldn't be surprised if the flight's cancelled already.'

'Don't say that, dear – *please.*'

They didn't speak again until the car had crossed over the river to Long Island.

'I arranged everything with the servants,' Mr Foster said. 'They're all going off today. I gave them half-pay for six weeks and told Walker I'd send him a telegram when we wanted them back.'

'Yes,' she said. 'He told me.'

'I'll move into the club tonight. It'll be a nice change staying at the club.'

'Yes, dear. I'll write to you.'

'I'll call in at the house occasionally to see that everything's all right and to pick up the mail.'

'But don't you really think Walker should stay there all the time to look after things?' she asked meekly.

'Nonsense. It's quite unnecessary. And anyway, I'd have to pay him full wages.'

'Oh yes,' she said. 'Of course.'

'What's more, you never know what people get up to when they're left alone in a house,' Mr Foster announced, and with that he took out a cigar and, after snipping off the end with a silver cutter, lit it with a gold lighter.

She sat still in the car with her hands clasped together tight under the rug.

'Will you write to me?' she asked.

'I'll see,' he said. 'But I doubt it. You know I don't hold with letter-writing unless there's something specific to say.'

'Yes, dear, I know. So don't you bother.'

They drove on, along Queen's Boulevard, and as they approached the flat marshland on which Idlewild is built, the fog began to thicken and the car had to slow down.

'Oh dear!' cried Mrs Foster. 'I'm *sure* I'm going to miss it now! What time is it?'

'Stop fussing,' the old man said. 'It doesn't matter anyway. It's bound to be cancelled now. They never fly in this sort of weather. I don't know why you bothered to come out.'

She couldn't be sure, but it seemed to her that there was suddenly a new note in his voice, and she turned to look at him. It was difficult to observe any change in his expression under all that hair. The mouth was what counted. She wished, as she had so often before, that she could see the mouth clearly. The eyes never showed anything except when he was in a rage.

'Of course,' he went on, 'if by any chance it *does* go, then I agree with you – you'll be certain to miss it now. Why don't you resign yourself to that?'

She turned away and peered through the window at the fog. It seemed to be getting thicker as they went along, and now she could only just make out the edge of the road and the margin of grassland beyond it. She knew that her husband was still looking at her. She glanced at him again, and this time she noticed with a kind of horror that he was staring intently at the little place in the corner of her left eye where she could feel the muscle twitching.

'Won't you?' he said.

'Won't I what?'

'Be sure to miss it now if it goes. We can't drive fast in this muck.'

He didn't speak to her any more after that. The car crawled on and on. The driver had a yellow lamp directed on to the edge of the road, and this helped him to keep going. Other lights, some white and some yellow, kept coming out of the fog towards them, and there was an especially bright one that followed close behind them all the time.

Suddenly, the driver stopped the car.

'There!' Mr Foster cried. 'We're stuck. I knew it.'

'No, sir,' the driver said, turning round. 'We made it. This is the airport.'

Without a word, Mrs Foster jumped out and hurried through the main entrance into the building. There was a mass of people inside, mostly disconsolate passengers standing around the ticket counters. She pushed her way through and spoke to the clerk.

'Yes,' he said. 'Your flight is temporarily postponed. But please don't go away. We're expecting this weather to clear any moment.'

She went back to her husband who was still sitting in the car and told him the news. 'But don't you wait, dear,' she said. 'There's no sense in that.'

'I won't,' he answered. 'So long as the driver can get me back. Can you get me back, driver?'

'I think so,' the man said.

'Is the luggage out?'

'Yes, sir.'

'Good-bye, dear,' Mrs Foster said, leaning into the car and giving her husband a small kiss on the coarse grey fur of his cheek.

'Good-bye,' he answered. 'Have a good trip.'

The car drove off, and Mrs Foster was left alone.

The rest of the day was a sort of nightmare for her. She sat for hour after hour on a bench, as close to the airline counter as possible, and every thirty minutes or so she would get up and ask the clerk if the situation had changed. She always received the same reply – that she must continue to wait, because the fog might blow away at any moment. It wasn't until after six in the evening that the loudspeakers finally announced that the flight had been postponed until eleven o'clock the next morning.

Mrs Foster didn't quite know what to do when she heard this news. She stayed sitting on her bench for at least another half-hour, wondering, in a tired, hazy sort of way, where she might go to spend the night. She hated to leave the airport. She didn't wish to see her husband. She was terrified that in one way or another he would eventually manage to prevent her from getting to France. She would have liked to remain just where she was, sitting on the bench the whole night through. That would be the safest. But she was already exhausted, and it didn't take her long to realize that this was a ridiculous thing for an elderly lady to do. So in the end she went to a phone and called the house.

Her husband, who was on the point of leaving for the club, answered it himself. She told him the news, and asked whether the servants were still there.

'They've all gone,' he said.

'In that case, dear, I'll just get myself a room some-where for the night. And don't you bother yourself about it at all.'

'That would be foolish,' he said. 'You've got a large house here at your disposal. Use it.'

'But, dear, it's *empty*.'

'Then I'll stay with you myself.'

'There's no food in the house. There's nothing.'

'Then eat before you come in. Don't be so stupid, woman. Everything you do, you seem to want to make a fuss about it.'

'Yes,' she said. 'I'm sorry. I'll get myself a sand-wich here, and then I'll come on in.'

Outside, the fog had cleared a little, but it was still a long, slow drive in the taxi, and she didn't arrive back at the house on Sixty-second Street until fairly late.

Her husband emerged from his study when he heard her coming in. 'Well,' he said, standing by the study door, 'how was Paris?'

'We leave at eleven in the morning,' she answered. 'It's definite.'

'You mean if the fog clears.'

'It's clearing now. There's a wind coming up.'

'You look tired,' he said. 'You must have had an anxious day.'

'It wasn't very comfortable. I think I'll go straight to bed.'

'I've ordered a car for the morning,' he said. 'Nine o'clock.'

'Oh, thank you, dear. And I certainly hope you're not going to bother to come all the way out again to see me off.'

'No,' he said slowly. 'I don't think I will. But there's no reason why you shouldn't drop me at the club on your way.'

She looked at him, and at that moment he seemed to be standing a long way off from her, beyond the same borderline. He was suddenly so small and far away that she couldn't be sure what he was doing, or what he was thinking, or even what he was.

'The club is downtown,' she said. 'It isn't on the way to the airport.'

'But you'll have plenty of time, my dear. Don't you want to drop me at the club?'

'Oh, yes – of course.'

'That's good. Then I'll see you in the morning at nine.'

She went up to her bedroom on the second floor, and she was so exhausted from her day that she fell asleep soon after she lay down.

Next morning, Mrs Foster was up early, and by eight-thirty she was downstairs and ready to leave.

Shortly after nine, her husband appeared. 'Did you make any coffee?' he asked.

'No, dear. I thought you'd get a nice breakfast at the club. The car is here. It's been waiting. I'm all ready to go.'

They were standing in the hall – they always seemed to be meeting in the hall nowadays – she with her hat and coat and purse, he in a curiously cut Edwardian jacket with high lapels.

'Your luggage?'

'It's at the airport.'

'Ah yes,' he said. 'Of course. And if you're going to take me to the club first, I suppose we'd better get going fairly soon, hadn't we?'

'Yes!' she cried. 'Oh, yes – *please*!'

'I'm just going to get a few cigars. I'll be right with you. You get in the car.'

She turned and went to where the chauffeur was standing, and he opened the car door for her as she approached.

'What time is it?' she asked him.

'About nine-fifteen.'

Mr Foster came out five minutes later, and watching him as he walked slowly down the steps, she noticed that his legs were like goat's legs in those narrow stovepipe trousers that he wore. As on the day before, he paused half-way down to sniff the air and to examine the sky. The weather was still not quite clear, but there was a wisp of sun coming through the mist.

'Perhaps you'll be lucky this time,' he said as he settled himself beside her in the car.

'Hurry, please,' she said to the chauffeur. 'Don't bother about the rug. I'll arrange the rug. Please get going. I'm late.'

The man went back to his seat behind the wheel and started the engine.

'*Just* a moment!' Mr Foster said suddenly. 'Hold it a moment, chauffeur, will you?'

'What is it, dear?' She saw him searching the pockets of his overcoat.

'I had a little present I wanted you to take to Ellen,' he said. 'Now, where on earth is it? I'm sure I had it in my hand as I came down.'

'I never saw you carrying anything. What sort of present?'

'A little box wrapped up in white paper. I forgot to give it to you yesterday. I don't want to forget it today.'

'A little box!' Mrs Foster cried. 'I never saw any little box!' She began hunting frantically in the back of the car.

Her husband continued searching through the pockets of his coat. Then he unbuttoned the coat and felt around in his jacket. 'Confound it,' he said, 'I must've left it in my bedroom. I won't be a moment.'

'Oh, *please*!' she cried. 'We haven't got time! *Please* leave it! You can mail it. It's only one of those silly combs anyway. You're always giving her combs.'

'And what's wrong with combs, may I ask?' he said, furious that she should have forgotten herself for once.

'Nothing, dear, I'm sure. But . . .'

'Stay here!' he commanded. 'I'm going to get it.'

'Be quick, dear! Oh, *please* be quick!'

She sat still, waiting and waiting.

'Chauffeur, what time is it?'

The man had a wristwatch, which he consulted. 'I make it nearly nine-thirty.'

'Can we get to the airport in an hour?'

'Just about.'

At this point, Mrs Foster suddenly spotted a corner of something white wedged down in the crack of the seat on the side where her husband had been sitting. She reached over and pulled out a small paper-wrapped box, and at the same time she couldn't help noticing that it was wedged down firm and deep, as though with the help of a pushing hand.

'Here it is!' she cried. 'I've found it! Oh dear, and now he'll be up there for ever searching for it! Chauffeur, quickly – run in and call him down, will you please?'

The chauffeur, a man with a small rebellious Irish mouth, didn't care very much for any of this, but he climbed out of the car and went up the steps to the front door of the house. Then he turned and came back. 'Door's locked,' he announced. 'You got a key?'

'Yes – wait a minute.' She began hunting madly in her purse. The little face was screwed up tight with anxiety, the lips pushed outward like a spout.

'Here it is! No – I'll go myself. It'll be quicker. I know where he'll be.'

She hurried out of the car and up the steps to the front door, holding the key in one hand. She slid the key into the keyhole and was about to turn it – and then she stopped. Her head came up, and she stood there absolutely motionless, her whole body arrested right in the middle of all this hurry to turn the key and get into the house, and she waited – five, six, seven, eight, nine, ten seconds, she waited. The way she was standing there, with her head in the air and the body so tense, it seemed as though she were listening for the repetition of some sound that she had heard a moment before from a place far away inside the house.

Yes – quite obviously she was listening. Her whole attitude was a *listening* one. She appeared actually to be moving one of her ears closer and closer to the door. Now it was right up against the door, and for still another few seconds she remained in that position, head up, ear to door, hand on key, about to enter but not entering, trying instead, or so it seemed, to hear and to analyse these sounds that were coming faintly from this place deep within the house.

Then, all at once, she sprang to life again. She withdrew the key from the door and came running back down the steps.

'It's too late!' she cried to the chauffeur. 'I can't wait for him, I simply can't. I'll miss the plane. Hurry now, driver, hurry! To the airport!'

The chauffeur, had he been watching her closely, might have noticed that her face had turned absolutely white and that the whole expression had suddenly altered. There was no longer that rather soft and silly look. A peculiar hardness had settled itself upon the features. The little mouth, usually so flabby, was now tight and thin, the eyes were bright, and the voice, when she spoke, carried a new note of authority.

'Hurry, driver, hurry!'

'Isn't your husband travelling with you?' the man asked, astonished.

'Certainly not! I was only going to drop him at the club. It won't matter. He'll understand. He'll get a cab. Don't sit there talking, man. *Get going*! I've got a plane to catch for Paris!'

With Mrs Foster urging him from the back seat, the man drove fast all the way, and she caught her plane with a few minutes to spare. Soon she was high up over the Atlantic, reclining comfortably in her aeroplane chair, listening to the hum of the motors, heading for Paris at last. The new mood was still with her. She felt remarkably strong and, in a queer sort of way, wonderful. She was a trifle breathless with it all, but this was more from pure astonishment at what she had done than anything else, and as the plane flew farther and farther away from New York and East Sixty-second Street, a great sense of calmness began to settle upon her. By the time she reached Paris, she was just as strong and cool as she could wish.

She met her grandchildren, and they were even more beautiful in the flesh than in their photographs. They were like angels, she told herself, so beautiful they were. And every day she took them for walks, and fed them cakes, and bought them presents, and told them charming stories.

Once a week, on Tuesdays, she wrote a letter to her husband – a nice, chatty letter – full of news and gossip, which always ended with the words 'Now be sure to take your meals regularly, dear, although this is something I'm afraid you may not be doing when I'm not with you.'

When six weeks were up, everybody was sad that she had to return to America, to her husband. Everybody, that is, except her. Surprisingly, she didn't seem to mind as much as one might have expected, and when she kissed them all good-bye, there was something in her manner and in the things she said that appeared to hint at the possibility of a return in the not too distant future.

However, like the faithful wife she was, she did not overstay her time. Exactly six weeks after she had arrived, she sent a cable to her husband and caught the plane back to New York.

Arriving at Idlewild, Mrs Foster was interested to observe that there was no car to meet her. It is possible that she might even have been a little amused. But she was extremely calm and did not overtip the porter who helped her into a taxi with her baggage.

New York was colder than Paris, and there were lumps of dirty snow lying in the gutters of the streets. The taxi drew up before the house on Sixty-second Street, and Mrs Foster persuaded the driver to carry her two large cases to the top of the steps. Then she paid him off and rang the bell. She waited, but there was no answer. Just to make sure, she rang again, and she could hear it tinkling shrilly far away in the pantry, at the back of the house. But still no one came.

So she took out her own key and opened the door herself.

The first thing she saw as she entered was a great pile of mail lying on the floor where it had fallen after being slipped through the letter box. The place was dark and cold. A dust sheet was still draped over the grandfather clock. In spite of the cold, the atmosphere was peculiarly oppressive, and there was a faint and curious odour in the air that she had never smelled before.

She walked quickly across the hall and disappeared for a moment around the corner to the left, at the back. There was something deliberate and purposeful about this action; she had the air of a woman who is off to investigate a rumour or to confirm a suspicion. And when she returned a few seconds later, there was a little glimmer of satisfaction on her face.

She paused in the centre of the hall, as though wondering what to do next. Then, suddenly, she turned and went across into her husband's study. On the desk she found his address book, and after hunting through it for a while she picked up the phone and dialled a number.

'Hello,' she said. 'Listen – this is Nine East Sixty-second Street . . . Yes, that's right. Could you send someone round as soon as possible, do you think? Yes, it seems to be stuck between the second and third floors. At least, that's where the indicator's pointing . . . Right away? Oh, that's very kind of you. You see, my legs aren't any too good for walking up a lot of stairs. Thank you so much. Good-bye.'

She replaced the receiver and sat there at her husband's desk, patiently waiting for the man who would be coming soon to repair the lift.

The Landlady

Billy Weaver had travelled down from London on the slow afternoon train, with a change at Swindon on the way, and by the time he got to Bath it was about nine o'clock in the evening and the moon was coming up out of a clear starry sky over the houses opposite the station entrance. But the air was deadly cold and the wind was like a flat blade of ice on his cheeks.

'Excuse me,' he said, 'but is there a fairly cheap hotel not too far away from here?'

'Try The Bell and Dragon,' the porter answered, pointing down the road. 'They might take you in. It's about a quarter of a mile along on the other side.'

Billy thanked him and picked up his suitcase and set out to walk the quarter-mile to The Bell and Dragon. He had never been to Bath before. He didn't know anyone who lived there. But Mr Greenslade at the Head Office in London had told him it was a splendid city. 'Find your own lodgings,' he had said, 'and then go along and report to the Branch Manager as soon as you've got yourself settled.'

Billy was seventeen years old. He was wearing a new navy-blue overcoat, a new brown trilby hat, and a new brown suit, and he was feeling fine. He walked briskly down the street. He was trying to do everything briskly these days. Briskness, he had decided, was *the* one common characteristic of all successful businessmen. The big shots up at Head Office were absolutely fantastically brisk all the time. They were amazing.

There were no shops on this wide street that he was walking along, only a line of tall houses on each side, all of them identical. They had porches and pillars and four or five steps going up to their front doors, and it was obvious that once upon a time they had been very swanky residences. But now, even in the darkness, he could see that the paint was peeling from the woodwork on their doors and windows, and that the handsome white façades were cracked and blotchy from neglect.

Suddenly, in a downstairs window that was brilliantly illuminated by a street-lamp not six yards away, Billy caught sight of a printed notice propped up against the glass in one of the upper panes. It said BED AND BREAKFAST. There was a vase of pussy-willows, tall and beautiful, standing just underneath the notice.

He stopped walking. He moved a bit closer. Green curtains (some sort of velvety material) were hanging down on either side of the window. The pussy-willows looked wonderful beside them. He went right up and peered through the glass into the room, and the first thing he saw was a bright fire burning in the hearth. On the carpet in front of the fire, a pretty little dachshund was curled up asleep with its nose tucked into its belly. The room itself, so far as he could see in the half-darkness, was filled with pleasant furniture. There was a baby-grand piano and a big sofa and several plump armchairs; and in one corner he spotted a large parrot in a cage. Animals were usually a good sign in a place like this, Billy told himself; and all in all, it looked to him as though it would be a pretty decent house to stay in. Certainly it would be more comfortable than The Bell and Dragon.

On the other hand, a pub would be more congenial than a boarding-house. There would be beer and darts in the evenings, and lots of people to talk to, and it would probably be a good bit cheaper, too. He had stayed a couple of nights in a pub once before and he had liked it. He had never stayed in any boarding-houses, and, to be perfectly honest, he was a tiny bit frightened of them. The name itself conjured up images of watery cabbage, rapacious landladies, and a powerful smell of kippers in the living-room.

After dithering about like this in the cold for two or three minutes. Billy decided that he would walk on and take a look at The Bell and Dragon before making up his mind. He turned to go.

And now a queer thing happened to him. He was in the act of stepping back and turning away from the window when all at once his eye was caught and held in the most peculiar manner by the small notice

that was there. BED AND BREAKFAST, it said. BED AND
BREAKFAST, BED AND BREAKFAST, BED AND BREAK-
FAST. Each word was like a large black eye staring at
him through the glass, holding him, compelling him,
forcing him to stay where he was and not to walk
away from that house, and the next thing he knew,
he was actually moving across from the window to
the front door of the house, climbing the steps that
led up to it, and reaching for the bell.

He pressed the bell. Far away in a back room he
heard it ringing, and then *at once* – it must have been
at once because he hadn't even had time to take his
finger from the bell-button – the door swung open
and a woman was standing there.

Normally you ring the bell and you have at least
a half-minute's wait before the door opens. But this
dame was like a jack-in-the-box. He pressed the bell
– and out she popped! It made him jump.

She was about forty-five or fifty years old, and the
moment she saw him, she gave him a warm welcoming smile.

'*Please* come in,' she said pleasantly. She stepped
aside, holding the door wide open, and Billy found
himself automatically starting forward into the house.
The compulsion or, more accurately, the desire to
follow after her into that house was extraordinarily
strong.

'I saw the notice in the window,' he said, holding
himself back.

'Yes, I know.'

'I was wondering about a room.'

'It's *all* ready for you, my dear,' she said. She had a round pink face and very gentle blue eyes.

'I was on my way to The Bell and Dragon,' Billy told her. 'But the notice in your window just happened to catch my eye.'

'My dear boy,' she said, 'why don't you come in out of the cold?'

'How much do you charge?'

'Five and sixpence a night, including breakfast.'

It was fantastically cheap. It was less than half of what he had been willing to pay.

'If that is too much,' she added, 'then perhaps I can reduce it just a tiny bit. Do you desire an egg for breakfast? Eggs are expensive at the moment. It would be sixpence less without the egg.'

'Five and sixpence is fine,' he answered. 'I should like very much to stay here.'

'I knew you would. Do come in.'

She seemed terribly nice. She looked exactly like the mother of one's best school-friend welcoming one into the house to stay for the Christmas holidays. Billy took off his hat, and stepped over the threshold.

'Just hang it there,' she said, 'and let me help you with your coat.'

There were no other hats or coats in the hall. There were no umbrellas, no walking-sticks – nothing.

'We have it *all* to ourselves,' she said, smiling at him over her shoulder as she led the way upstairs.

'You see, it isn't very often I have the pleasure of taking a visitor into my little nest.'

The old girl is slightly dotty, Billy told himself. But at five and sixpence a night, who gives a damn about that? 'I should've thought you'd be simply swamped with applicants,' he said politely.

'Oh, I am, my dear, I am, of course I am. But the trouble is that I'm inclined to be just a teeny weeny bit choosy and particular – if you see what I mean.'

'Ah, yes.'

'But I'm always ready. Everything is always ready day and night in this house just on the off-chance that an acceptable young gentleman will come along. And it is such a pleasure, my dear, such a very great pleasure when now and again I open the door and I see someone standing there who is just *exactly* right.' She was half-way up the stairs, and she paused with one hand on the stair-rail, turning her head and smiling down at him with pale lips. 'Like you,' she added, and her blue eyes travelled slowly all the way down the length of Billy's body, to his feet, and then up again.

On the first-floor landing she said to him, 'This floor is mine.'

They climbed up a second flight. 'And this one is *all* yours,' she said. 'Here's your room. I do hope you'll like it.' She took him into a small but charming front bedroom, switching on the light as she went in.

'The morning sun comes right in the window, Mr Perkins. It *is* Mr Perkins, isn't it?'

'No,' he said. 'It's Weaver.'

'Mr Weaver. How nice. I've put a water-bottle between the sheets to air them out, Mr Weaver. It's such a comfort to have a hot water-bottle in a strange bed with clean sheets, don't you agree? And you may light the gas fire at any time if you feel chilly.'

'Thank you,' Billy said. 'Thank you ever so much.' He noticed that the bedspread had been taken off the bed, and that the bedclothes had been neatly turned back on one side, all ready for someone to get in.

'I'm so glad you appeared,' she said, looking earnestly into his face. 'I was beginning to get worried.'

'That's all right,' Billy answered brightly. 'You mustn't worry about me.' He put his suitcase on the chair and started to open it.

'And what about supper, my dear? Did you manage to get anything to eat before you came here?'

'I'm not a bit hungry, thank you,' he said. 'I think I'll just go to bed as soon as possible because tomorrow I've got to get up rather early and report to the office.'

'Very well, then. I'll leave you now so that you can unpack. But before you go to bed, would you be kind enough to pop into the sitting-room on the ground floor and sign the book? Everyone has to do that because it's the law of the land, and we don't want to go breaking any laws at *this* stage of the proceedings, do we?' She gave him a little wave of the hand

and went quickly out of the room and closed the door.

Now, the fact that his landlady appeared to be slightly off her rocker didn't worry Billy in the least. After all, she was not only harmless – there was no question about that – but she was also quite obviously a kind and generous soul. He guessed that she had probably lost a son in the war, or something like that, and had never got over it.

So a few minutes later, after unpacking his suitcase and washing his hands, he trotted downstairs to the ground floor and entered the living-room. His landlady wasn't there, but the fire was glowing in the hearth, and the little dachshund was still sleeping in front of it. The room was wonderfully warm and cosy. I'm a lucky fellow, he thought, rubbing his hands. This is a bit of all right.

He found the guest-book lying open on the piano, so he took out his pen and wrote down his name and address. There were only two other entries above his on the page, and, as one always does with guest-books, he started to read them. One was a Christopher Mulholland from Cardiff. The other was Gregory W. Temple from Bristol.

That's funny, he thought suddenly. Christopher Mulholland. It rings a bell.

Now where on earth had he heard that rather unusual name before?

Was he a boy at school? No. Was it one of his sister's numerous young men, perhaps, or a friend of his father's? No, no, it wasn't any of those. He glanced down again at the book.

Christopher Mulholland   231 *Cathedral Road, Cardiff*
Gregory W. Temple   27 *Sycamore Drive, Bristol*

As a matter of fact, now he came to think of it, he wasn't at all sure that the second name didn't have almost as much of a familiar ring about it as the first.

'Gregory Temple?' he said aloud, searching his memory. 'Christopher Mulholland? . . .'

'Such charming boys,' a voice behind him answered, and he turned and saw his landlady sailing into the room with a large silver tea-tray in her hands. She was holding it well out in front of her, and rather high up, as though the tray were a pair of reins on a frisky horse.

'They sound somehow familiar,' he said.

'They do? How interesting.'

'I'm almost positive I've heard those names before somewhere. Isn't that queer? Maybe it was in the newspapers. They weren't famous in any way, were they? I mean famous cricketers or footballers or something like that?'

'Famous,' she said, setting the tea-tray down on the low table in front of the sofa. 'Oh no, I don't think they were famous. But they were extraordinarily handsome, both of them, I can promise you that. They were tall and young and handsome, my dear, just exactly like you.'

Once more, Billy glanced down at the book. 'Look

here,' he said, noticing the dates. 'This last entry is over two years old.'

'It is?'

'Yes, indeed. And Christopher Mulholland's is nearly a year before that – more than *three years* ago.'

'Dear me,' she said, shaking her head and heaving a dainty little sigh. 'I would never have thought it. How time does fly away from us all, doesn't it, Mr Wilkins?'

'It's Weaver,' Billy said. 'W-e-a-v-e-r.'

'Oh, of course it is!' she cried, sitting down on the sofa. 'How silly of me. I do apologize. In one ear and out the other, that's me, Mr Weaver.'

'You know something?' Billy said. 'Something that's really quite extraordinary about all this?'

'No, dear, I don't.'

'Well, you see – both of these names, Mulholland and Temple, I not only seem to remember each one of them separately, so to speak, but somehow or other, in some peculiar way, they both appear to be sort of connected together as well. As though they were both famous for the same sort of thing, if you see what I mean – like . . . well . . . like Dempsey and Tunney, for example, or Churchill and Roosevelt.'

'How amusing,' she said. 'but come over here now, dear, and sit down beside me on the sofa and I'll give you a nice cup of tea and a ginger biscuit before you go to bed.'

'You really shouldn't bother,' Billy said. 'I didn't mean you to do anything like that.' He stood by the piano, watching her as she fussed about with the cups and saucers. He noticed that she had small, white, quickly moving hands, and red finger-nails.

'I'm almost positive it was in the newspapers I saw them,' Billy said. 'I'll think of it in a second. I'm sure I will.'

There is nothing more tantalizing than a thing like this which lingers just outside the borders of one's memory. He hated to give up.

'Now wait a minute,' he said. 'Wait just a minute. Mulholland . . . Christopher Mulholland . . . wasn't *that* the name of the Eton schoolboy who was on a walking-tour through the West Country, and then all of a sudden . . .'

'Milk?' she said. 'And sugar?'

'Yes, please. And then all of a sudden . . .'

'Eton schoolboy?' she said. 'Oh no, my dear, that can't possibly be right because *my* Mr Mulholland was certainly not an Eton schoolboy when he came to me. He was a Cambridge undergraduate. Come over here now and sit next to me and warm yourself in front of this lovely fire. Come on. Your tea's all ready for you.' She patted the empty place beside her on the sofa, and she sat there smiling at Billy and waiting for him to come over.

He crossed the room slowly, and sat down on the edge of the sofa. She placed his teacup on the table in front of him.

'*There* we are,' she said. 'How nice and cosy this is, isn't it?'

Billy started sipping his tea. She did the same. For half a minute or so, neither of them spoke. But Billy knew that she was looking at him. Her body was half-turned towards him, and he could feel her eyes resting on his face, watching him over the rim of her teacup. Now and again, he caught a whiff of a peculiar smell that seemed to emanate directly from her person. It was not in the least unpleasant, and it reminded him – well, he wasn't quite sure what it reminded him of. Pickled walnuts? New leather? Or was it the corridors of a hospital?

'Mr Mulholland was a great one for his tea,' she said at length. 'Never in my life have I seen anyone drink as much tea as dear, sweet Mr Mulholland.'

'I suppose he left fairly recently,' Billy said. He was still puzzling his head about the two names. He was positive now that he had seen them in the newspapers – in the headlines.

'Left?' she said, arching her brows. 'But my dear boy, he never left. He's still here. Mr Temple is also here. They're on the third floor, both of them together.'

Billy set down his cup slowly on the table, and stared at his landlady. She smiled back at him, and then she put out one of her white hands and patted him comfortingly on the knee. 'How old are you, my dear?' she asked.

'Seventeen.'

'Seventeen!' she cried. 'Oh, it's the perfect age! Mr Mulholland was also seventeen. But I think he was a trifle shorter than you are, in fact I'm sure he was, and his teeth weren't *quite* so white. You have the most beautiful teeth, Mr Weaver, did you know that?'

'They're not as good as they look,' Billy said. 'They've got simply masses of fillings in them at the back.'

'Mr Temple, of course, was a little older,' she said, ignoring his remark. 'He was actually twenty-eight. And yet I never would have guessed it if he hadn't told me, never in my whole life. There wasn't a *blemish* on his body.'

'A what?' Billy said.

'His skin was *just* like a baby's.'

There was a pause. Billy picked up his teacup and took another sip of his tea, then he set it down again gently in its saucer. He waited for her to say something else, but she seemed to have lapsed into another of her silences. He sat there staring straight ahead of him into the far corner of the room, biting his lower lip.

'That parrot,' he said at last. 'You know something? It had me completely fooled when I first saw it through the window from the street. I could have sworn it was alive.'

'Alas, no longer.'

'It's most terribly clever the way it's been done,' he said. 'It doesn't look in the least bit dead. Who did it?'

'I did.'

'*You* did?'

'Of course,' she said. 'And you have met my little Basil as well?' She nodded towards the dachshund curled up so comfortably in front of the fire. Billy looked at it. And suddenly, he realized that this animal had all the time been just as silent and motionless as the parrot. He put out a hand and touched it gently on the top of its back. The back was hard and cold, and when he pushed the hair to one side with his fingers, he could see the skin underneath, greyish-black and dry and perfectly preserved.

'Good gracious me,' he said. 'How absolutely fascinating.' He turned away from the dog and stared with deep admiration at the little woman beside him on the sofa. 'It must be most awfully difficult to do a thing like that.'

'Not in the least,' she said. 'I stuff *all* my little pets myself when they pass away. Will you have another cup of tea?'

'No, thank you,' Billy said. The tea tasted faintly of bitter almonds, and he didn't much care for it.

'You did sign the book, didn't you?'

'Oh, yes.'

'That's good. Because later on, if I happen to forget what you were called, then I can always come down here and look it up. I still do that almost every day with Mr Mulholland and Mr . . . Mr . . .'

'Temple,' Billy said. 'Gregory Temple. Excuse my asking, but haven't there been *any* other guests here except them in the last two or three years?'

Holding her teacup high in one hand, inclining her head slightly to the left, she looked up at him out of the corners of her eyes and gave him another gentle little smile.

'No, my dear,' she said. 'Only you.'

POCKET PENGUINS

36. **Muriel Spark** The Snobs
37. **Steven Pinker** Hotheads
38. **Tony Harrison** Under the Clock
39. **John Updike** Three Trips
40. **Will Self** Design Faults in the Volvo 760 Turbo
41. **H. G. Wells** The Country of the Blind
42. **Noam Chomsky** Doctrines and Visions
43. **Jamie Oliver** Something for the Weekend
44. **Virginia Woolf** Street Haunting
45. **Zadie Smith** Martha and Hanwell
46. **John Mortimer** The Scales of Justice
47. **F. Scott Fitzgerald** The Diamond as Big as the Ritz
48. **Roger McGough** The State of Poetry
49. **Ian Kershaw** Death in the Bunker
50. **Gabriel García Márquez** Seventeen Poisoned Englishmen
51. **Steven Runciman** The Assault on Jerusalem
52. **Sue Townsend** The Queen in Hell Close
53. **Primo Levi** Iron Potassium Nickel
54. **Alistair Cooke** Letters from Four Seasons
55. **William Boyd** Protobiography
56. **Robert Graves** Caligula
57. **Melissa Bank** The Worst Thing a Suburban Girl Could Imagine
58. **Truman Capote** My Side of the Matter
59. **David Lodge** Scenes of Academic Life
60. **Anton Chekhov** The Kiss
61. **Claire Tomalin** Young Bysshe
62. **David Cannadine** The Aristocratic Adventurer
63. **P. G. Wodehouse** Jeeves and the Impending Doom
64. **Franz Kafka** The Great Wall of China
65. **Dave Eggers** Short Short Stories
66. **Evelyn Waugh** The Coronation of Haile Selassie
67. **Pat Barker** War Talk
68. **Jonathan Coe** 9th & 13th
69. **John Steinbeck** Murder
70. **Alain de Botton** On Seeing and Noticing